For all those who have been, and continue to be,
touched by dementia. Especially our very wonderful
Veronica Spry
— C. H. W.

For my Granny Teasie and Barbara Anne
— A. L.

tiger tales
5 River Road, Suite 128, Wilton, CT 06897
Published in the United States 2019
Originally published in Great Britain 2019
by Little Tiger Press Ltd.
Text copyright © 2019 Clare Helen Welsh
Illustrations copyright © 2019 Ashling Lindsay
ISBN-13: 978-1-68010-141-6
ISBN-10: 1-68010-141-2
Printed in China
LTP/1400/2415/0918

For more insight and activities, visit us at www.tigertalesbooks.com

The Tide

by Clare Helen Welsh   Illustrated by Ashling Lindsay

tiger tales

Sometimes, Grandpa forgets things.
Like he did the day we went to the beach
and watched the tide come in.

Mommy says that Grandpa loves me very much but that sometimes, he gets confused.

She says it must be annoying to forget how to do things, and I agreed.

Like the time I couldn't remember how to tie my shoes, and my teacher helped me.

So when we're at the beach,
I hold Grandpa's hand.

We build forts and castles.

We are the king and queen
of sand and shells . . .
and we watch the tide come in.

We have a picnic in the sun . . .

but where are all the sandwiches?

I love my grandpa, but sometimes, I get upset when he does silly things.

I try to remember that it must be scary to forget.

Like the time I
buried Polar Bear,
and Mommy helped
me find him.

So when we're at the beach, I give
Grandpa a big hug and kiss.

We search for sleepy sea stars.
We jump from pool to pool . . .

and we watch the
tide come in.

But what if Grandpa forgets ME?

It must be scary to forget someone you love.
I haven't ever forgotten somebody that important.

Mommy says Grandpa's memories are like the tide.
Sometimes, they're near and full of life.

Other times, they're distant and quiet.

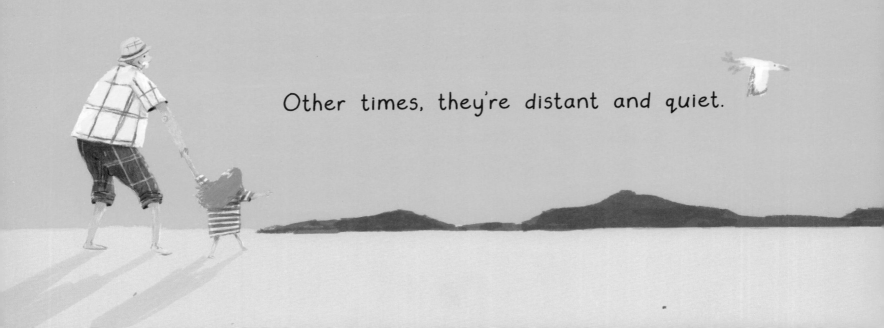

But I know that he loves me more
than lapping waves and sandy toes
on sunny days.

All of a sudden, we hear voices!
Happy, laughing voices;
everybody smiles.

But Grandpa's smile is the biggest.
We gather our coins and pennies.
We savor every lick . . .

and we watch the tide.

But the tide is in!

We dip our startled toes. We dance through rolling waves.
Because the tide is in!

We shower in the spray. We wave at smiling gulls.
Because the tide is in!

Then we empty out our pockets,
and dry our sandy clothes.

We wash our salty skin,
then snuggle nice and close . . .

. . . to talk about the day we watched the tide come in.

Because Grandpa doesn't remember
things like he used to.

But I love him as much as I always have.
And I know that he loves me.